The Old Man and T

A true story written and illustrated by

Richard Schlatter

The Old Man and The Tree, Published October, 2014

Interior and Cover Illustrations: Richard Schlatter
Interior Layout: Howard Johnson, Howard Communigrafix, Inc.
Editorial and Proofreading: Eden Rivers Editorial Services
Photo Credit: Linda Schlatter

 SDP Publishing

Published by SDP Publishing, an imprint of SDP Publishing Solutions, LLC.

For more information about this book contact Lisa Akoury-Ross by email at lross@SDPPublishing.com.

ISBN-13 (print): 978-0-9913167-8-6
ISBN-13 (ebook): 978-0-9913167-9-3

Printed in the United States of America

JAXON –
DON'T CUT DOWN
YOUR FRIENDS.

[signature]

:)

I would like to dedicate this book
to my grandchildren, Addison and Brayton,
who inspired me to publish this story.

Fred was still a young man when he bought his house on Applewood Lane.

And in the backyard, there was a young maple tree.

Fred thought, "Gee, it would be nice if that tree was a little bigger to give me some shade."

The tree was near Fred's patio.
Fred planted plants and flowers around it,
which made his house look nice.

Then one day, Fred built a room on his patio and added a deck. He built a small pond with a waterfall next to his deck right under the maple tree.

7

At night, Fred put a spotlight at the base of the tree to show its beautiful form and graceful branches. Fred and the tree were becoming good friends.

9

Fred really liked the tree. After many years,
the tree was big enough to give him lots
of shade on hot, summer days. And in the
fall, the tree's leaves became a beautiful,
colorful shade of yellow.

As Fred got older, so did the tree.
They kind of grew old together.

12

Even though he liked the tree, Fred noticed that the tree had some bad habits. Every spring, it would cough up thousands of little seeds that floated to the ground like tiny helicopters.

This caused Fred great discomfort
because he had to climb up on his roof
and clean the seeds out of his gutters.

Fred was getting older, and climbing up
and down the ladder was hard work.
But if he didn't, water would come
through the basement windows and
flood his basement.

As the years passed, Fred became more bothered by the tree's bad habits—the helicopters in the spring increased. So did the dead leaves in the fall, which made the deck slippery when they got wet.

The tree said to Fred, "Many years ago, you wished that I was bigger so I could give you shade. Now I am, and you are unhappy with me."

"I know," said Fred, "but I am getting old, and it is hard for me to clean up your mess every spring and every fall. It's getting harder for me to take care of you. I have no choice but to get rid of you."

The next day, Fred called a tree man to come and cut down his old friend the maple tree. When Fred heard the sound of the buzzing chain saw, he left his house because he could not watch his friend being cut down.

When Fred came home, he was sad—very sad. His longtime friend, the maple tree, was gone. The only thing left was a stump.

The tree was gone, and so was the shade. Old Fred's deck was now hot and sunny in the afternoon. Fred realized that even though the tree had some bad habits, it was still a good friend. Now it was gone. Forever.

Fred walked over to the big stump and sat down. He thought about the many years they spent together. He thought about the shade that the tree gave him during the hot, summer months. He thought about the home it provided for the songbirds like the cardinals and chickadees.

He thought about the beautiful color it gave him in the fall. He asked himself, "Why did I get rid of such a good friend just because he had a few bad habits?"

Fred continued to think, "What if my friends cut me down or got rid of me because of my bad habits?"

Fred felt sick. He knew he made a mistake. But it was too late. His friend, the maple tree, was gone. Now that Fred was an old man he realized that it took a lifetime to build a friendship, but one bad decision ended that friendship forever.

The old man continued to sit on the stump in the hot sun. He looked down at the ground and saw a small helicopter from the tree. He picked it up and wished that he had his old friend back.

Then, he had an idea. He put the seed
in a pot of dirt and watered it every day.
Soon, a small maple tree began to grow.

The following spring, the old man planted the
little tree near where the old maple tree once
stood. He hoped that someday, somebody
else would enjoy its shade in the summer, its
bright color in the fall, and the sweet sounds
of the songbirds perched on its branches.

The End

About The Author

Richard Schlatter studied architecture, art, and design at the University of Cincinnati, and graphic design and photography at the Ray-Vogue schools in Chicago. After a three-year stint working for a Chicago art studio, he moved to Michigan and became the art director of an advertising agency in Battle Creek. He formed SchlatterDesign in 1972, a full-service design firm, and still works as an independent advertising/graphic design consultant.

His first children's book, *The Old Man and The Tree*, is a true story. The author recalls, "After cutting down a large maple tree near my house, I felt depressed and knew I made a mistake. I wanted my tree back, but it was too late. When I shared the experience with my six-year-old granddaughter, she inspired me to write the story and get it published."

Richard lives in Battle Creek with his wife, Linda, and their two rescue cats.

CPSIA information can be obtained
at www.ICGtesting.com
Printed in the USA
LVHW051237150223
739406LV00002B/3

9 780991 316786